Bob the Builder

Bob's Egg and Spoon Race

One sunny morning, the machines noticed that Bob and Wendy were acting strangely.

"Oh, er – what's Bob doing running down the road balancing an egg on a spoon?" asked Muck.

"I don't know," chuckled Dizzy, "but Wendy's doing the same thing."

"Whooaaa!" called Roley. "Watch out!"

Crash!

"Are you OK, Bob?" Wendy asked, picking herself up.

"Fine, thanks," said Bob. "No bones broken, and look...no eggs broken, either."

"Er, Bob," said Muck, "why didn't your eggs smash?"

"Because they are hard-boiled," Bob explained. "We're using them to practise for the egg and spoon race."

Mr Sabatini was making a giant pizza for the winner of the race. It was part of the town Fun Day that Mrs Percival was organizing.

"That's enough practice, Bob. We'd better go and put in the new doors at the Pizza Parlour," said Wendy.

4

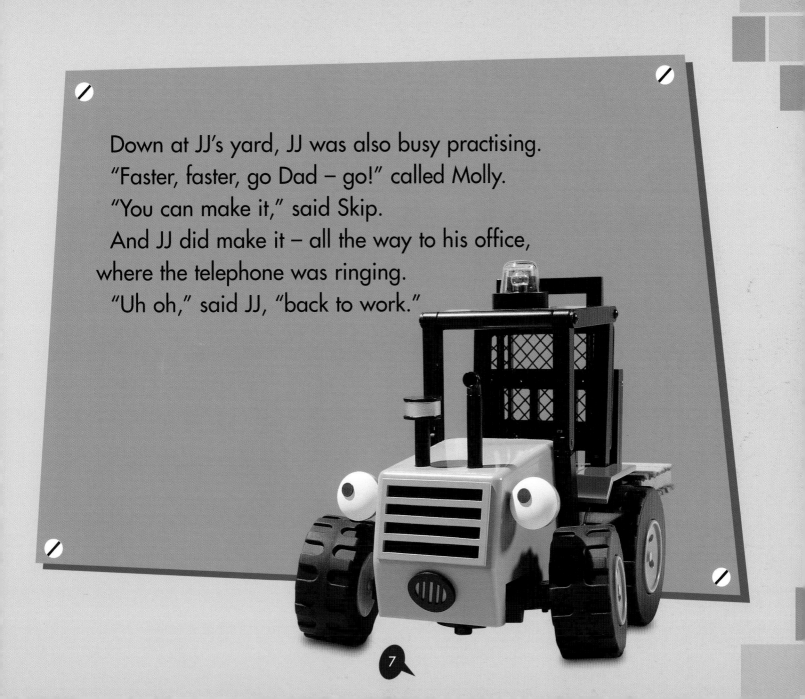

Down at JJ's yard, JJ was also busy practising.
"Faster, faster, go Dad – go!" called Molly.
"You can make it," said Skip.
And JJ did make it – all the way to his office,
where the telephone was ringing.
"Uh oh," said JJ, "back to work."

Over at Farmer Pickles's farm, Spud was complaining.

"All I ever do is carry eggs," he said, as he was given another tray of freshly-laid eggs.

"That's because everyone needs eggs to practise for the race," said Farmer Pickles.

"Yeah, well I'm going to win that race," said Spud, "because I want to eat that giant pizza."

"Hello," said Spud when he got to JJ's yard. "Farmer Pickles sent these eggs for JJ."

"Great!" said Trix. "More for me to practise with."

"But Trix, they're for JJ," said Spud.

"Go on Spud – just one – please?" said Trix.

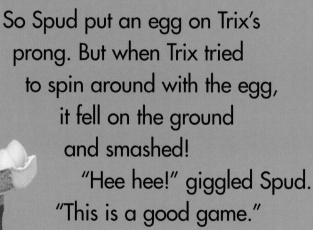

So Spud put an egg on Trix's prong. But when Trix tried to spin around with the egg, it fell on the ground and smashed!

"Hee hee!" giggled Spud. "This is a good game."

"I just don't understand it," Trix said. "Before, the eggs sort of…bounced."

"What on earth's been going on here?" said JJ, as he and Molly came out of the office.

"Sorry," said Trix. "These eggs from Farmer Pickles keep breaking."

"That's because they are fresh eggs," explained JJ. "You were using hard-boiled eggs before."

Over at the pizza shop, Mr Sabatini rushed out with a smile on his face.

"Oh, Wendy!" he said. "My new place is looking fantastic…and the pizza prize is cooking beautifully."

"Mmmmmmm! I can smell it," said Bob.

"It's a good job you're putting in those smart double doors," said Mr Sabatini.

"Why's that?" asked Wendy.

"Well, I'd have trouble getting the giant pizza out," joked Mr Sabatini.

"Let's get started on the doors," said Bob. "**Can we fix it?**" he called to the machines.

"**Yes we can!**" they called back.

First, Bob and Wendy put the spare bricks in a skip. Then Trix carried the new door frame and glass from JJ's yard. Soon, the frame was in place, and Wendy put the glass in, using sticky putty.

No one saw Spud creep up and take some putty.

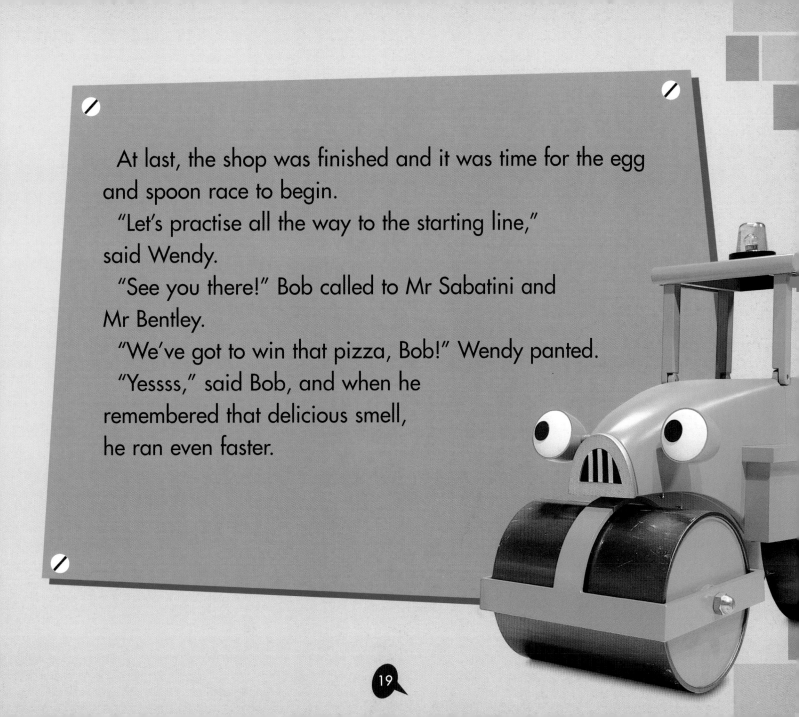

At last, the shop was finished and it was time for the egg and spoon race to begin.

"Let's practise all the way to the starting line," said Wendy.

"See you there!" Bob called to Mr Sabatini and Mr Bentley.

"We've got to win that pizza, Bob!" Wendy panted.

"Yessss," said Bob, and when he remembered that delicious smell, he ran even faster.

Mrs Percival was waiting at the starting line. She asked everyone to place their egg on their spoon.

Then she called, "On your marks…get set…GO!" and everyone sprinted off.

The tricky part was running at the same time as balancing the egg on the spoon.

JJ turned to Trix. "Remember, Trix – control!"

"I'll try, JJ!" said Trix, shaking completely out of control.

Spud wasn't in the lead to begin with, but when everyone else slowed down for the bend in the road, Spud kept up the same speed.

"Look at me!" called Spud. "Lah, lah, la-lah!"

Mrs Potts dropped her egg as Spud ran past her.

Trix was really trying her best, but she just couldn't keep the egg on her prong and keep up with Spud.

"Yummieeeeeee!" cried Spud as he raced over the finishing line.

"Well done, Spud – that was amazing," praised Bob.

"Hurray!" called Muck and Dizzy.

"Yummy! I've won the giant pizza!" whooped Spud, swinging the spoon around. Strangely, the egg stayed on the spoon.

"Spud," said Bob. "How did you do that?"

Mrs Percival came running up. "Spud," she asked, "what's underneath your egg?"

Spud blushed. "Ooh! I used a bit of sticky stuff to stop my egg falling off."

"But that's cheating," said Mrs Percival.

"I'm really sorry, Mrs Percival," said Spud.

"Spud is out of the race," she announced. "So…let me see, yes… Trix is the winner."

"Hurray!" called Muck and Dizzy again. Spud looked sad.

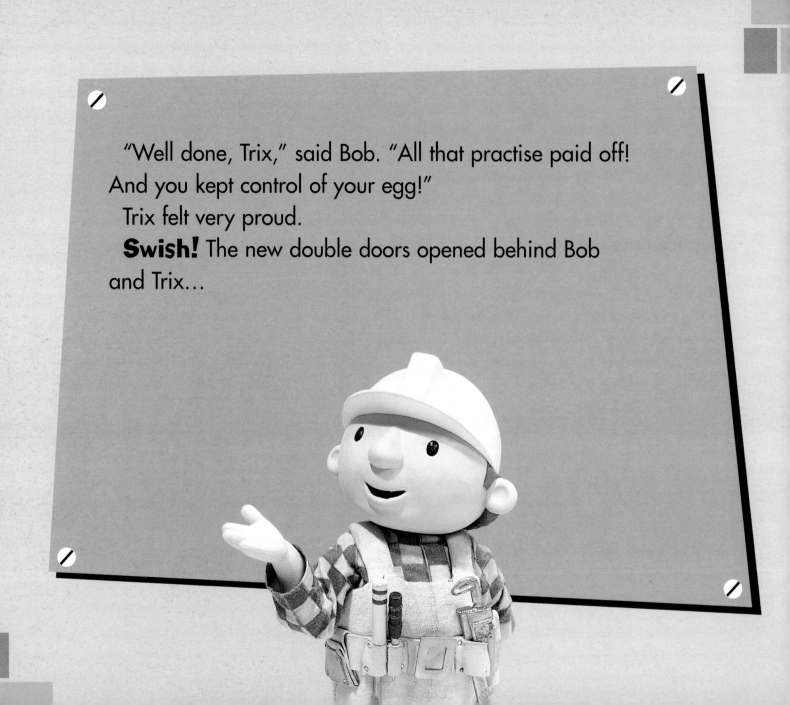

"Well done, Trix," said Bob. "All that practise paid off! And you kept control of your egg!"

Trix felt very proud.

Swish! The new double doors opened behind Bob and Trix…

…and there was Mr Sabatini with the giant pizza.

"Here she is!" he announced. "And bravo to the egg and spoon race winner – Trix!"

Trix moved towards the doors, lowered her prongs, picked up the pizza, and smoothly backed up with it.

"There's a slice for everyone!" said Trix. "Tuck in."

Spud didn't think this included him, but when Trix gave him a wink, he raced forwards to grab the first slice.

"Oh, thanks, Trix!" said Spud.
"I see your egg still hasn't fallen off your spoon," joked Bob. Everyone laughed except Spud, who was too busy eating the wonderful pizza.

THE END!